Y0-CDP-652

BETTER SOCCER

for Boys and Girls

BETTER SOCCER
for Boys and Girls

George Sullivan

G.P. PUTNAM'S SONS · NEW YORK

The author is grateful to the many people who helped him in the preparation of this book. Special thanks are offered Chuck Florea, vice president and senior division coach, Brookside Soccer Club, Springfield, Massachusetts, for his interest and cooperation, and to these members of the club who posed for photographs: Jeff Bates, Jon Bates, Tim Bates, Luigi Calabrese, Karen Calvanese, Susan Calvanese, Daimon Ciavola, Fred Ciavola, Mary Ellen Donegan, Darrin Edwards, Rick Hanchett, Don Howe, Pat Kearney, John Martel, Steven Olson, Jeff Pouliot, James Sciartelli, Joseph Sciartelli, Donna Skawski, and Ray Wholley. The author is also grateful to Gary Wagner, Wagner-International Photos; Herb Field, Herb Field Studios; Aime LaMontagne, Tim Sullivan, and Bill Sullivan.

PICTURE CREDITS

New York Public Library, 8; Tim Sullivan, 6, 23 (right), 49, 50, 51. All other photographs are by George Sullivan.

 Published in 1989 by G.P. Putnam's Sons, a Division of The Putnam & Grosset Group, 200 Madison Avenue, New York, New York 10016. Originally published in 1978 by Dodd, Mead & Co., Inc. Published simultaneously in Canada. Printed in the United States of America.

Library of Congress Cataloging-in-Publication Data
Sullivan, George, 1927- Better soccer for boys and girls. Summary: Discusses the rules, equipment, and techniques of soccer, the fastest-growing team sport in the United States. 1. Soccer – Juvenile literature. [1. Soccer] I. Title. GV943.25.S94 1989 796.334'2 88-32393 ISBN 0-399-61232-7
10 9 8 7 6

CONTENTS

Soccer excitement and fun on a summer afternoon.

AS AMERICAN AS BASEBALL

When Joe Camilleri, coach of the Bergen Kickers, a sandlot soccer team from Leonia, New Jersey, organized the team in 1970, he had to plead for players. Only 15 youngsters showed up for the first tryout. But now there are more than 100 boys who turn out each season when Camilleri issues a call for new talent.

In Greece, New York, a suburb of Rochester, where there once were four baseball diamonds and no soccer fields in a neighborhood park, there are now three soccer fields and but one surviving baseball diamond.

These two pieces of evidence give an idea of what's been happening with soccer in recent years. Simply stated, soccer is the fastest-growing team sport in the United States. Or, as *The New York Times* noted in 1977, soccer is "suddenly something as American as, say, baseball."

It's not difficult to understand why soccer has become so popular as a participant sport:

- There are no size requirements. You don't have to be tall. You don't have to be big.
- Girls play the game as easily as boys. Experience and coaching are what are important. "When young girls get a chance to learn the fundamentals, practice, and be in game situations, they frequently outshine boy players," says one coach. "After all, their skills develop sooner. Only if the boys get bigger and stronger do they have an advantage."
- It's an inexpensive sport. A ball and a level place to play are about all that are required. "I can outfit a player for about $25 a season," says another junior coach. "Make it $50 if we include warm-up jackets and practice uniforms. You can't buy a football helmet for that."
- Soccer is a good conditioner. All that running that young players do gets the heart and lungs in shape for their life's work. The health benefits of soccer also relate to the sport's injury rate, which is low. Compared to football and hockey, it's *very* low.
- And, most important, soccer is fun. There's no waiting around for something to happen, as there is in baseball. The action is continuous. "You get to the ball just by running to it," says one young player. "And you can be like the quarterback every time you kick the ball."

As regards soccer vs. football, a ten-year-old Rahway, New Jersey, boy offers this argument: "You don't have those crazy coaches yelling 'stick-'em! hit-'em!' all the time. You don't have all those big guys jumping on you. I'm a polite little kid."

A coach for a Rockville Center, New York, team has yet another reason why the sport is proving so popular. "All the members of the team know who's doing the job out there," he says. "And when they play a game, everyone has a feeling of accomplishment. It's as simple as that."

By the mid-nineteenth century, soccer had spread to the four corners of the globe. This is a scene in Manila in the 1850s.

Soccer is one of the oldest known sports. Over a thousand years ago, the Greeks and Romans played games in which one team tried to kick an inflated ball over a goal line defended by an opposition team.

Roman soldiers are said to have introduced the game to England. It eventually became so popular there that in 1349 King Edward III came to look upon the game as a threat to England's security. He wanted his subjects to spend their time practicing archery, since skill with the bow and arrow was vital to the nation's defense.

The king called soccer "an idle pastime." He ordered his sheriffs to ban the game, but the people continued to play.

In those days, games lasted many hours and were set up at the opposite ends of the main streets of hamlets or towns. Players were permitted to kick an opponent's shins or trip. You could, in fact, do about anything you wanted to get the ball over the goal or keep it from a member of the opposition team.

Modern soccer—that is, a version of the game that resembles soccer as it is played today—dates to

1863, the year that the London Football Association published its rules.

The London Football Association also gave the game its official name: Association Football. The word soccer is thought to be derived from Association, or from assoc., the abbreviated form of the word.

Soccer mushroomed in popularity in England, and was transported to every corner of the globe by English sailors, soldiers, and settlers. In 1904, the Federation Internationale de Football Association (FIFA) was founded, with France, Belgium, Switzerland, Holland, and Denmark represented.

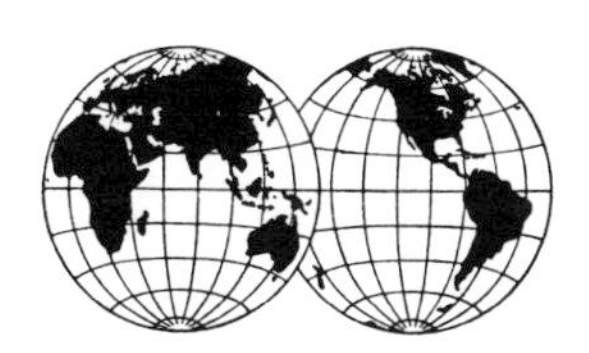

FIFA

FIFA helped make soccer rules uniform all over the world. No matter what nations they represent, teams are able to play one another on an equal footing. And playing the game gives one a sense of the world community.

Soccer was slow to develop in the United States. Waves of immigrants who came to America during the 1880s, and had learned soccer in their homelands, brought the game with them. So soccer came to be a game identified with "foreigners"—Germans and Poles, Italians and Irish, Greeks and Hungarians.

Native Americans, meanwhile, had sports of their own to play and watch, first baseball, later football and basketball. For nearly a hundred years, soccer had a stepchild status on the American sports scene.

The situation began to change during the 1960s. Two rival professional leagues sought to set up shop in 1967. The result was a disaster, but out of that disaster came the 19-team North American Soccer League (NASL), which one day was to rival the long-established football and baseball leagues in terms of both esteem and popularity.

Interest in soccer among school-age youngsters has been growing steadily for several years. Once the game began to become successful on a professional level, the number of young participants took a dramatic jump. The first draft of college players took place in 1972. In other words, young American players could begin thinking in terms of a future in soccer for the first time.

The professional version of the game also gave American fans their first soccer stars. Pelé, for instance, frequently called the greatest soccer player of all time. Pelé was thirty-four when, in 1975, he came out of retirement to join the NASL's New York Cosmos. He received a contract reported to be worth $4.5 million over a three-year period.

Born in the Brazilian town of Tres Coracoes

Pelé unlimbers with Cosmos teammates.

(Three Hearts), Pelé played his first soccer barefoot and kicking a ball of rags in the city streets. He was playing junior soccer at the age of twelve, and three years later he joined the Santos Futebol Clube, where he was to earn his greatest fame.

From the very beginning, Pelé awed opponents with his grace, explosive speed, and amazing ball control skills. He could pluck a line-drive out of the air, and have control of the ball before it hit the ground. He could rebound the ball off an opponent's legs, or slip it between them and pick it up on the other side. When he dribbled the ball, it seemed to be tied to his legs with a piece of string.

Pelé had an uncanny awareness of the movements of both his teammates and the opposition players, and was a clever and cunning passer as a result. He had a sixth sense about the weaknesses of goalies, and in his 18-year career with the Santos team scored 1,220 goals in 1,253 games, an average of almost one a game.

Pelé's most memorable feat occurred in the World Cup tournament. The national teams of approximately 140 countries compete in the World Cup matches, sponsored by FIFA and held every four years. Pelé, as a member of the 1958 Brazilian team, scored a three-goal "hat trick" against France in the semifinal round. In the championship game against Sweden, he scored twice in Brazil's 5-2 victory. It was Brazil's first World Cup win and established Pelé as a national resource on a par with the coffee bean. Pelé was seventeen at the time.

The World Cup victory in 1958 marked the beginning of Brazil's dominance in international soccer competition for the next twelve years, with Pelé leading the way. The Brazilians won the World Cup in 1962 and again in 1970.

Pelé quit soccer in 1974. Afterward, he received lucrative offers from many countries seeking to lure him out of retirement. Soccer fans around the world were stunned when Pelé chose to resume his career with an American team. Pelé explained the reasoning behind his decision: "If the offer to play had been from a team in England, West Germany or Spain, or any other country besides the United States, I would have refused. But here, I might be able to improve the level of soccer."

Pelé was very sincere in this aim. At clinics for young players, Pelé was always an earnest participant. And when, in the summer of 1977, the Cosmos drew a record 62,394 spectators to their stadium in East Rutherford, New Jersey, for a game against the Tampa Bay Rowdies, there was no one happier than Pelé. His enthusiasm that day stemmed in part from the fact that he scored three goals, as the Cosmos won, 3-1.

Pelé gives words of advice at Cosmos clinic.

In 1977, his final year with the team, Pelé often shared headlines with other international stars the Cosmos had signed—Italy's Giorgio Chinaglia and West Germany's Franz Beckenbauer. Pelé, Chinaglia, and Beckenbauer were the three principal reasons the Cosmos averaged more than 35,000 fans per game, the highest average in the league. This was a far cry from a time several years before when the general manager of the Cosmos had called a meeting of the team's fan club, and only two people showed up. That's because the fan club had only two members.

Statistics showing what's happened to youth soccer in recent years are just as glowing. The United States Soccer Federation (USSF), the governing body of American soccer, administers the United States Youth Soccer Association (USYSA) for boys and girls ages seven through eighteen. There were 30,000 youngsters enrolled in the program in 1972. By 1977, the number was 228,000.

The rival American Youth Soccer Organization

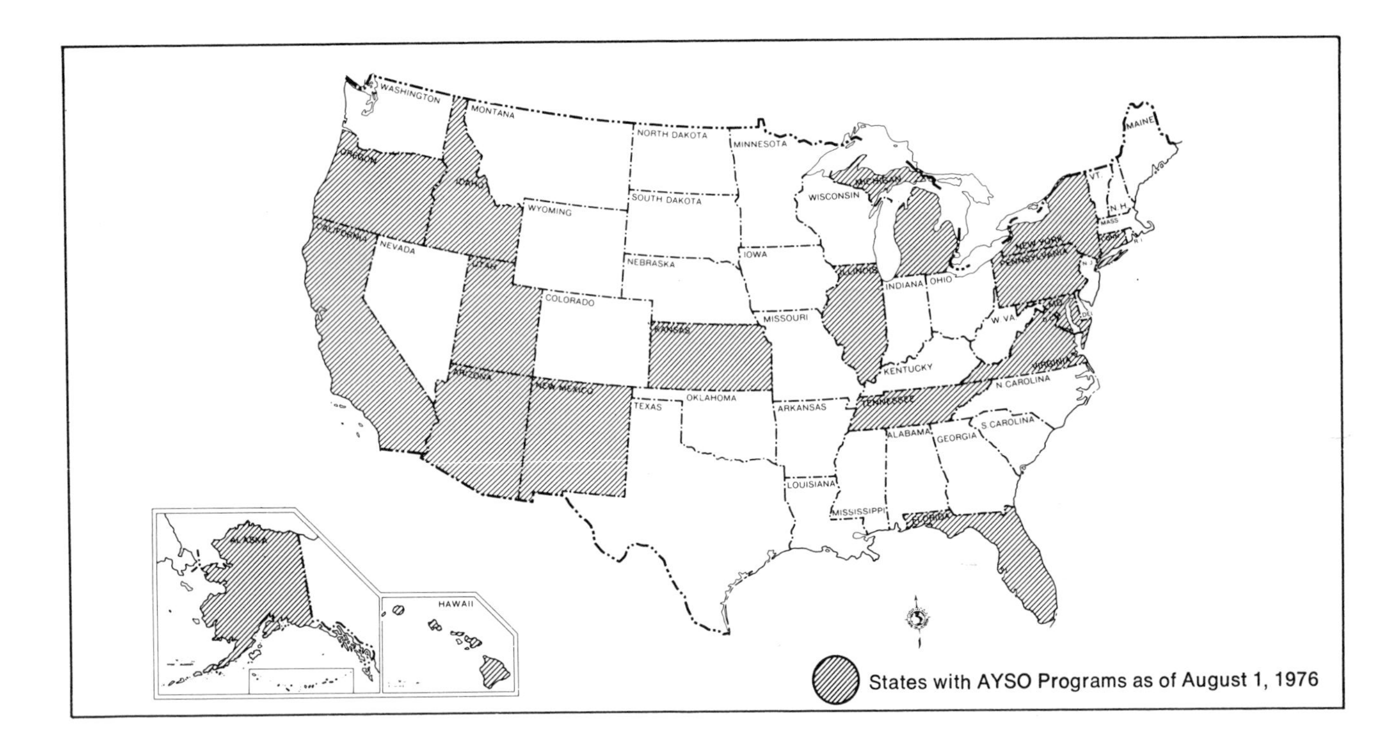

(AYSO) began operation in 1964 with eight boys' teams. Today the California-based organization, active in approximately 20 states, has 9,000 teams, with girls making up about 25 percent of the membership.

The combined registration figures indicated that approximately 350,000 youths ages eighteen and under were playing organized soccer during 1977. But the sport is much more popular than these figures imply, for they do not reflect the tens of thousands of public and private schools, YMCAs and YWCAs, and park and recreation departments that offer soccer programs. The best estimate is that about two million boys and girls are kicking that checkered sphere over broad, grassy surfaces. And more than a few people agree that this may be only the beginning, that one day soccer will rank as the favorite sport of American youths, bar none.

HOW THE GAME IS PLAYED

Soccer's simplicity is one reason that it is the most popular sport in the world. Play is continuous. Opposing teams move from one end of the field and back, with the flow halted only when the ball goes out of bounds, when there is a penalty, or when a goal is scored. Each goal is worth 1 point. The team that gets the most goals wins. The game is exactly the same in more than 140 countries.

The soccer field is a rectangle, with its dimensions permitted to vary within certain limits. The length can be from 100 yards to 130 yards. The width can vary from 50 yards to 100 yards. (For players under twelve, smaller fields are recommended, but a field can never be less than 40 yards by 80 yards.)

The end lines are called goal lines, and the goals are set in the middle of each. The sidelines are called touchlines. A halfway line across the center of the field divides it in half.

Other dimensions are as follows:

Goal: 8 yards wide, 8 feet high. (For players under twelve, goals that are 7 yards wide and 7 feet high are recommended.)

Goal area: 20 yards wide, 6 yards deep.

Penalty area: 44 yards wide, 18 yards deep.

Penalty spot: in front of the goal, 12 yards from the goal line.

Penalty arc: a radius of 10 yards from the penalty spot.

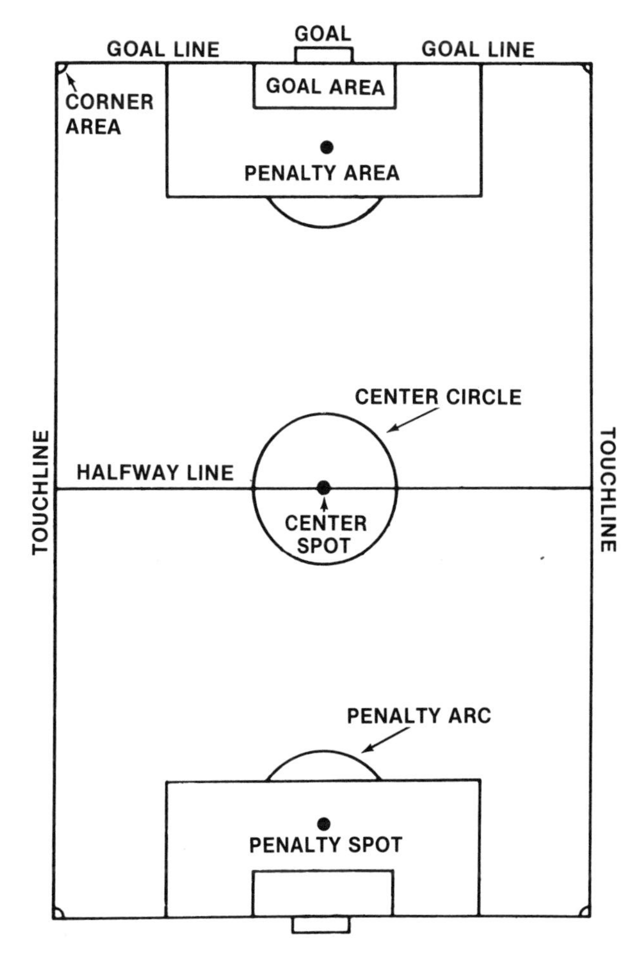

Center circle: a radius of 10 yards from the center spot, the center of the field.

Corner area: a radius of 1 yard with the corner.

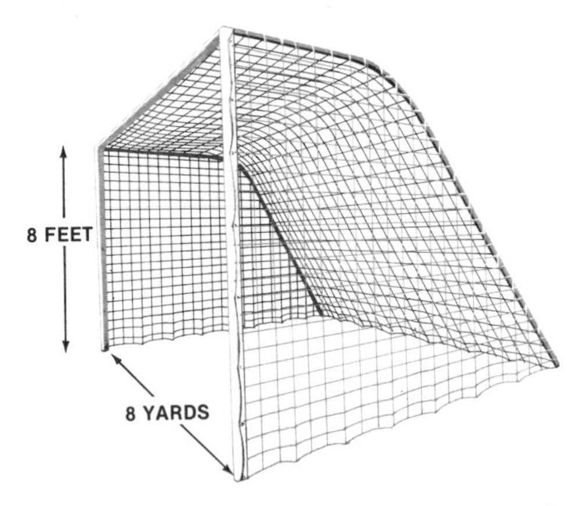

Net portion of goal is made of hand-knotted cotton or nylon cord.

An official game for adults lasts 90 minutes. It's played in 45-minute halves, with a 5- or 10-minute interval. For young players, games are of shorter duration:

AGE	LENGTH OF GAME
Under 16	Two 40-minute halves
Under 14	Two 35-minute halves
Under 12	Two 30-minute halves
Under 10	Two 25-minute halves

Play is supervised by a referee who is sometimes assisted by two linesmen. The linesmen, using small flags, indicate where the ball has gone out of bounds, and they award goal kicks, corner kicks, and throw-ins (see below). Each linesman is responsible for half the field. In high school games and most junior competition, two referees usually officiate.

There are 11 players on a team. They try to get the ball into the opponent's goal. Only one member of each team, the goalkeeper, is permitted to catch

Soccer play is supervised by a referee (left). Right: Linesmen—there are two of them—assist the referee, each one responsible for half the field.

or throw the ball. The other 10 members can kick the ball, butt it with the head, or block it with the body.

A coin toss decides which team begins the game by kicking off. The team that wins the toss has the choice of either kicking off or selecting the goal it wishes to defend.

On a signal from the referee, a player kicks the ball from the center spot into the opponent's half of the field. Each player must be within his team's half of the field and defensive players must be at least 10 yards from the ball.

A similar kickoff is used to put the ball in play after a goal has been scored. If team A has scored, a player from team B kicks off.

If, during the course of a game, the ball goes over a touchline, the same rule that is common to basketball applies. If the ball was last touched by team A, then it is put back in play by a member of team B. This is done by a throw-in. The hands *are* used when throwing in. (The throw-in is discussed in detail later in this book; see contents page.)

If the ball goes over the goal line (but not into the goal), and was last played by the attacking team, it is put back into play with a goal kick. A member of the defending team takes the goal kick from a point within the goal area. He kicks the ball upfield through the penalty area. No member of the offensive team is permitted within the penalty area at the time the kick is executed.

A throw-in is the method of restarting play after the ball has gone out of bounds.

If the defending team causes the ball to go over its goal line, the ball is put back in play with a corner kick. In this, the ball is placed down within the cor-

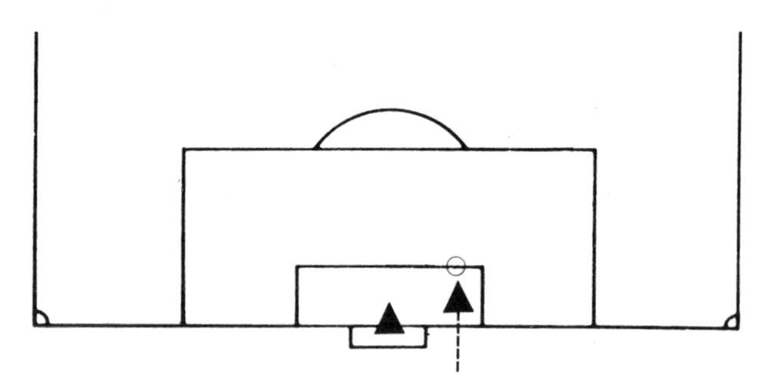

A goal kick

ner area closest to where the ball crossed the goal line, and is kicked by a member of the offensive team. Defensive team members must stay at least 10 yards away.

There are nine major fouls in soccer. Handling the ball intentionally is one of them. Using the hands to hold, push, or strike an opponent also results in a major foul.

The feet can get a player into foul trouble, too.

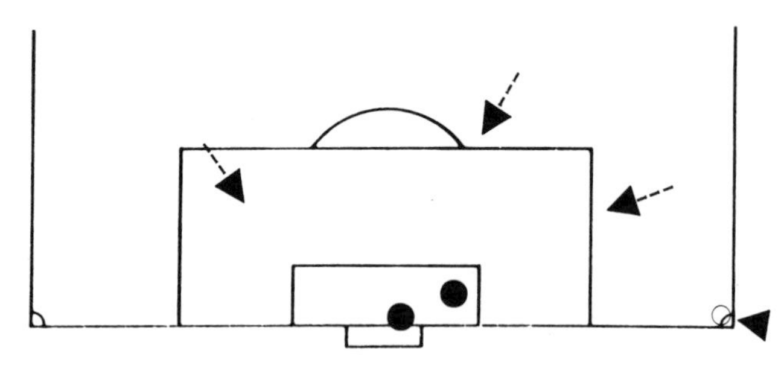

A corner kick

You cannot trip, kick, or jump an opponent. The other two fouls concern charging. You are not permitted to charge in "a dangerous or violent manner," nor are you permitted to charge an opponent from behind.

Should a member of team A be guilty of one of these fouls, a member of team B is given a direct free kick. It takes place from the point of infraction. Players on team A must be at least 10 yards from the ball at the time the kick is executed. A goal may be scored on a direct free kick.

If any one of the nine major fouls cited above is committed by a defending team within its own penalty area, the team attacking is awarded a penalty kick. After the ball is placed on the penalty spot, a player on the attacking team takes a shot at the goal. No other player from either team is permitted within the penalty area. In other words, only the goalkeeper is allowed to defend against the kick, and he is not permitted to move his feet until the ball has been kicked. In professional soccer, the kicker almost always scores in penalty-kick situations.

Penalties are also given for any one of several minor offenses. These include intentionally obstructing an opponent, dangerous play, or coaching from the sidelines.

In such cases, the penalty is an indirect free kick against the offending team. Like the direct free kick, the indirect free kick is taken from the point of the infraction and opposing players must stay at least 10

Charging from behind—a free kick for the opposition.

yards away from the ball. The difference is that a goal cannot be scored directly. The kicker must first kick the ball to another player.

Another infraction for which an indirect free kick is awarded is being offside. Soccer's offside rule can be difficult to understand. Keep in mind its purpose. Just as is the case with the offside rule in hockey, it is meant to prevent offensive players from hanging around the goalmouth, waiting for a pass.

The offside rule states that when the ball is passed to an attacking player, there must be at least two defensive players (the goalkeeper, usually, and one

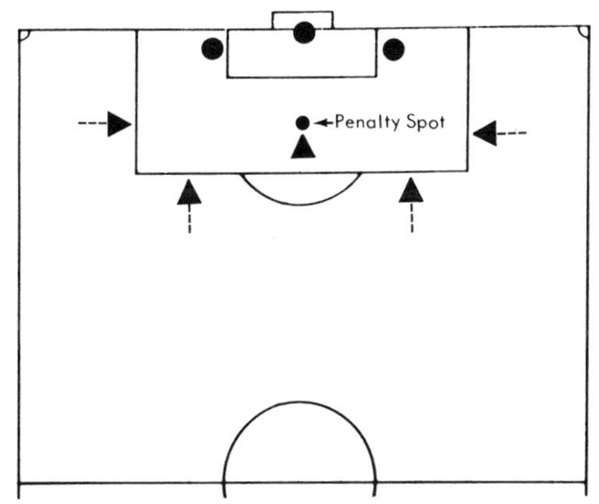

A penalty kick

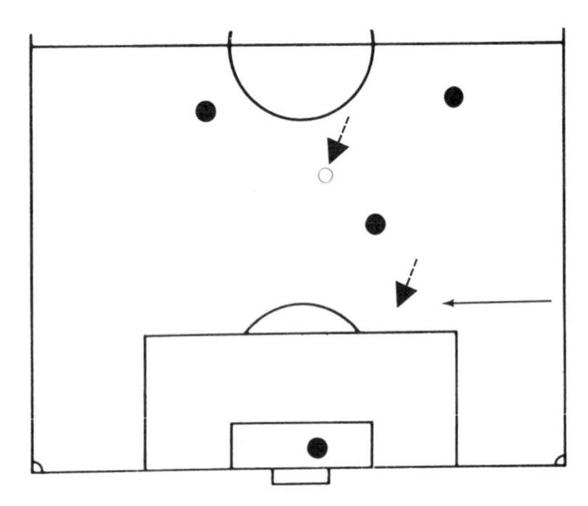

Arrow at right indicates player offside.

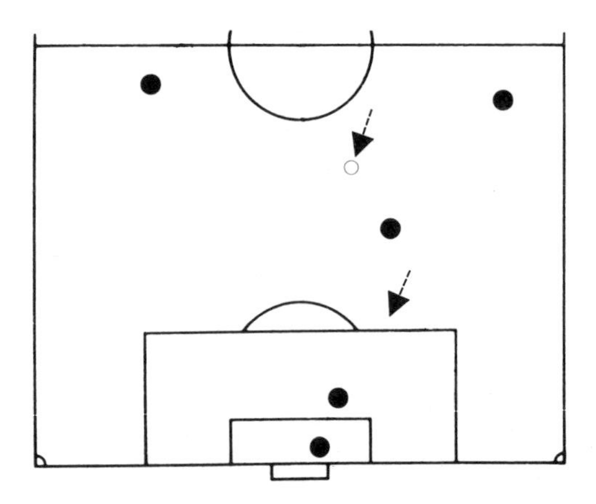

There's no offside here, because two defensive players are positioned between the offensive player and the goal.

other player) between him and the goal line.

The rule applies only in the opponent's half of the field. In other words, an intended pass receiver can never be offside in his own half of the field.

In the North American Soccer League, it's different. Yellow lines are drawn across each end of the field, 35 yards from each goal line. Offside violations are called only within the area between a yellow line and a goal line.

In both amateur and professional play, a player cannot be offside in receiving the ball after it first touches a defending player. Nor is there an offside violation when a player receives the ball directly from a goal kick, a corner kick, or a throw-in.

While in professional soccer and most amateur adult play, substitutions are rare, in junior soccer, they are, to quote the rulebook, "unlimited."

The rules for boys' and girls' soccer are exactly the same, with one exception: girls are permitted to use their arms to protect the upper part of their bodies.

For a detailed presentation of the rules, get a copy of *Illustrated Soccer Rules*, which costs 50 cents. It can be obtained by writing the United States Soccer Federation (350 Fifth Avenue, Suite 4010, New York, N.Y. 10001).

Soccer ball is constructed of 32 five-sided panels.

EQUIPMENT

Soccer requires only a ball. You can buy a ball that will last for two seasons of heavy play for about $15.

The ball is made of 32 five-sided black and white panels. These help a player to perceive the speed and direction of the ball's spin when it is in motion.

Balls vary in size. Players from thirteen to nineteen use a ball that's 27 to 28 inches in circumference and weighs from 14 to 16 ounces. Equipment stores refer to this as a size 5.

Youngsters from eight to twelve years of age use a ball that is from 25 to 26 inches in circumference, and weighs from 11 to 13 ounces—a size 4. Players younger than eight use a size 3 ball, which is 24 to 25 inches in circumference.

As a beginner, you can wear sneakers. But once you become serious about the game, you'll want to own a pair of soccer shoes. Modern soccer shoes are light in weight and cut below the ankle. Get a pair with a padded ankle collar, padded tongue, and a cushioned insole. Soccer shoes cost from $15 to $30 a pair.

The sole and heel are fittted with circular molded-rubber studs. The number can vary from as few as 6 to as many as 14. The studs provide traction.

Knee socks are frequently of stretch nylon. They have a turnover cuff at the top.

Some young players like to wear shin guards, which protect them from opposing kickers who miss the ball. They're worn under the knee socks and held in place by them. A pair of shin guards costs about $5.

Hard-rubber or plastic studs provide traction.

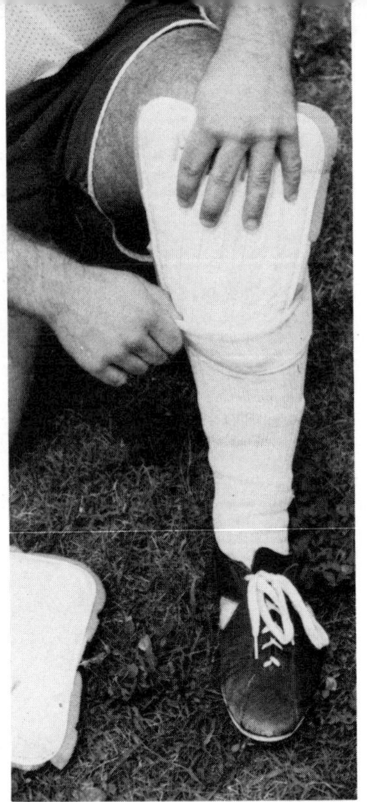

Soccer gear includes socks with a turnover cuff, shin guards that slip beneath socks, long-sleeved jerseys for cold weather, and gloves for the goalie on cold or wet days.

The rest of the soccer uniform consists of a nylon or cotton jersey, which is short-sleeved in the summer, long-sleeved in the winter. Goalies usually wear long-sleeved shirts the year-round for protection.

Soccer shorts are available in either nylon or cotton, too. The shorts have an elastic waistband that is fitted with a drawstring.

The goalie's uniform is not the same as his teammates'. He wears different colors so he can easily be spotted. For example, if a team wears a blue uniform with red trim, its goalie might wear a yellow and black uniform.

When the field is wet or the day is cold, the goalie is likely to wear gloves. They not only help to keep his hands warm, but they prevent the ball from slipping through his grasp.

RUNNING

Kicking, dribbling, heading, and trapping are the skills usually associated with soccer (and each is the subject of a section of this book). However, running is as important as any of these, perhaps more important. In any given soccer game, you will spend about 75 percent of your time running. This section is meant to help you improve your efficiency as a runner.

Never try to run at full speed without warming up first. This is especially true in cold weather. Plan to spend 10 to 15 minutes loosening up your muscles. When you fail to do this, you increase the risk of suffering a painful muscle pull.

Exercises like these help players unlimber.

In this muscle-stretching exercise, one player attempts to lift his leg while the other exerts pressure in the opposite direction.

Do some stretching exercises first. Bend from the waist with your feet apart, putting your palms to the ground. Keep your knees straight. Do this several times.

Push-ups and sit-ups are standard warm-up exercises.

With your hands on your hips, your feet apart, lean back from the waist. Lean to one side, then the other. Rotate your hips as if you were keeping a hula hoop in the air.

Lie on your back and do some leg spreads. With your legs straight out, your feet together, raise the legs off the ground slightly, and then spread them as far apart as you can. Push-ups and sit-ups are other good warm-up exercises.

Jog in position for about 30 seconds, then do some leg kicks. From a standing position, kick as high as you can, first with one leg, then the other. Spend about 30 seconds on this drill.

When your muscles are loose, jog the length of the field. Then jog in the other direction, gradually increasing your speed.

No two people run exactly alike. Each has a style of his own. So don't copy anyone's technique. Develop your own style, following the general advice set down here.

When you run, always keep your body erect. Stride on the balls of your feet. This will make it easier for you to start, stop, and change direction during a game.

Point your feet straight ahead. Reach out with your toes on each stride. Make each stride as long as you can.

Your rear leg should always start swinging forward before the front foot makes contact with the ground. In other words, the body "floats" in the air with both feet off the ground for a split second. There is never a period that both feet are on the ground at the same time.

Lift your knees forcefully with each stride. Generally speaking, the longer your strides and the higher you lift your knees, the faster you will go.

Keep your shoulders steady, but pump your arms

Keep your body erect as you run.

Make your strides as long as you can.

When you're running right, both feet come off the ground at the same time; you "float."

Swinging your arms helps increase your speed.

back and forth. This helps to increase speed, too. Keep your arms close to your body, that is, control their movement. If you let them swing wildly, you might accidentally hit the ball—and that can result in a penalty call.

Breathe through both the mouth and the nose while you're moving.

When you have a good distance to travel, build your speed gradually. It may take you as many as 10 to 12 strides to reach full speed.

KICKING

Kicking is soccer's basic skill. When you know how to kick, you're able to pass the ball accurately and shoot with power, and do both of these in a variety of game situations.

Soccer players almost never use the toes in executing a kick. Instead, the instep—the top of the foot where the shoe is laced—is used in striking the ball. The ball is also kicked with the inner and outer sides of the foot, and you can also punch the ball with the heel.

As a general rule, you rely on an instep kick when you want power. Use the inside of the foot for accuracy.

To be a good soccer player, you must become equally skilled with either foot. If you're naturally right-footed, kicking with the left foot may feel awkward at first. But with practice you'll overcome the awkward feeling.

In European countries, young soccer players sometimes set off for school in the morning with a soccer ball at their feet, kicking it as they go. They practice kicking on the way home from school, too.

While it may not be convenient for you to do this, you should practice kicking as frequently and as often as you can. Practice off a wall. Kick the ball toward the wall, then kick the rebound back. Move close to the wall; move back. Vary the types of kicks.

Next, practice kicking a moving ball. Kick the ball out in front of you, and before it stops kick it again. Use one foot and then the other. Keep changing the direction of your kicks, and occasionally approach the ball from across the path it's traveling, that is, from the side rather than from the rear.

Practice with a partner, the two of you kicking the ball back and forth. If you have a wall you can use, try this drill: As you approach the wall straight in front, a distance of 10 or 12 yards, have your partner kick the ball to you from one side. In order to get away a good shot, you'll have to time your approach properly, then pivot on your nonkicking foot in order to swing the other leg through. This drill duplicates a game situation you'll frequently encounter.

Never kick the ball aimlessly when you practice. Always try to have a target in mind, whether it be a teammate, a spot on the practice wall, or the goal. Unless you follow this policy, you'll never become accurate with your kicks.

There are several different types of kicks that you should know how to execute, and the paragraphs that follow explain them.

THE LOW DRIVE—The low drive, an instep kick, produces the type of shot that goalkeepers fear the most. The low drive can also be used for passing.

The "secret" to keeping the ball low is in placing your nonkicking foot alongside the ball—not behind it—as you swing the other foot through. This places your body over the ball, assuring you'll get the utmost power, but little loft.

In kicking the low drive, use your instep.

At the moment your instep makes contact, the knee of your kicking leg should be directly above the ball, or even slightly in front of it. The toes should be pointing downward as the foot swings through. Aim at the very center of the ball.

You must concentrate on the ball. If you lift your head to look at your target or if you're distracted by an opponent, your kick isn't likely to be an accurate one. Don't look up until the ball is on its way.

Always make an effort to swing your foot through the ball. Your kicking foot should be pointing at the target after the ball has been booted. If you pull your foot across the line, you'll hook the shot.

The first time you try a low drive (or any of the other shots described in this section), execute it from

The nonkicking foot is planted beside—not to the rear—of the ball.

Be sure to follow through.

a stationary position. Place a ball on the ground. Take one step back from it and stand with your feet together, your right foot slightly ahead of your left. Stride forward with your left foot, planting it alongside the ball. Swing the right instep through. Repeat the drill, but this time stride with the right foot, kicking with the left.

When you're able to kick with power and accuracy from a stationary position, try running and kicking. Go back three or four steps, and then run and kick the ball. Be sure to plant the nonkicking foot alongside the ball, not behind it. Keep your chin down, your eyes glued to the ball until the kick is executed.

When you become skilled in executing a low drive as described above, you can then try kicking the ball in such a way that it will veer to the right or left. Kicking the ball off-center is what makes it curve. To make the ball curve to the right, aim to the left of the ball's center. Use the outside of the right foot. To make the ball curve to the left, do the reverse.

In either case, you must approach the ball straight on. And you must kick decisively.

Why make the ball curve? It's a method of passing or shooting to use when a defending player threatens to intercept. You curve the ball around the player. But this is not a skill that a beginner should seek to develop. If you're in that category, concentrate on the standard low drive instead.

THE LOFTED DRIVE—This is a long-distance kick, again executed with the instep, but this time you lift the ball high into the air.

As you approach, plant your nonkicking foot slightly behind the ball and to the side of it. Make

To loft the ball, get your instep under the ball as you kick.

Plant your nonkicking foot behind the ball, not beside it, when you want to put the ball in the air.

contact below the center of the ball, using the lower half of your instep. In other words, your foot will be slightly underneath the ball as you make contact.

Lean backward slightly as you execute this kick. This helps to assure an upward swing as your foot comes through, and an upward swing is what gets the ball into the air.

Again, remember to concentrate on the ball. Follow through. Your toes should end up pointing in the direction the ball takes.

CHIPPING—In golf, a chip is a short approach shot that pops into the air and plops down onto the green. A chip in soccer is much the same, a shot that rises sharply, soaring over an opponent who may be only six or seven yards away.

The shot is executed in somewhat the same manner as the lofted drive. But instead of pointing your toes downward as you make contact, keep your kicking foot level to the ground. Slip the toes beneath the ball, and scoop it up. Lean back as you kick. Deftness is what's needed, not power.

Practice chipping by standing a few yards away from a partner. Put the ball at your feet and practice chipping it into the partner's upstretched hands.

INSIDE-OF-THE-FOOT KICK—When you want accuracy rather than power, use the inside-of-the-foot kick. It's the type of kick most often used for a pass of up to 15 to 20 yards.

Come straight through with your kicking leg.

In chipping the ball—getting it high in the air—you must slip your toes beneath the ball.

When passing, the inside-of-the-foot kick is frequently used.

Place your nonkicking foot alongside the ball. Turn your kicking foot outward as you swing it through. It should be at almost right angles to the ball as it makes contact.

Aim for the very center of the ball with the middle of the foot. Be sure to follow through.

OUTSIDE-OF-THE-FOOT KICK—While kicks executed with the outside of the foot are sure to lack in power, they're useful in certain types of passing. Suppose you're moving the ball downfield with your

You can also pass using the outside of the foot.

right foot, and there's a teammate on your right. Kicking the ball without breaking stride with a quick and deceptive flick of your right foot is the best way to get the ball to that teammate.

As you kick, turn the toe of the kicking foot inward. Part of your instep, as well as the side of the foot, will be involved in the kick. Follow through in the direction you want the ball to go.

VOLLEY AND HALF-VOLLEY—The terms volley and half-volley are used to describe different types of kicks. You can use any part of your foot in executing these kicks, except the toes.

The volley is a kick that's executed when the ball is in midair. Exactly how you volley depends on the height of the ball, its speed and direction.

In cases where the ball is coming directly toward you and is about knee level, lean back slightly as you move to kick. There's no time for a long windup. Simply swing your foot into the ball, making contact with your instep.

When you have an opportunity to shoot, your volley has to be more controlled. You want to drive the ball, not merely send it soaring. Stand to one side of the ball's path as it comes toward you, and lift your kicking leg so it will meet the ball on a horizontal plane. You swing your leg through, the way a baseball player whips the bat into the ball. Use your hands and arms to help pivot your body around. Pivoting is what puts power into the shot.

Some players have difficulty volleying because

Volleying a ball that's waist high.

they're unable to raise the kicking leg to hip level quickly enough. Practice this with a hurdle or stack of boxes, anything that will give you the right amount of height. Standing next to the hurdle, simply practice swinging your leg over it.

You can practice volley kicks by holding a ball in front of your body at about chest level, dropping it, and volleying it with either foot before it strikes the ground. Or you can toss the ball into the air, allow it to bounce, and then volley it. A more challenging drill is to toss the ball into the air and volley it before it touches the ground.

When performing these exercises, remember to point the toes of your kicking foot toward the ground. This serves to give you the largest surface possible with which to make contact with the ball.

When the ball is high in the air, at head level or higher, use an overhead volley. It's an acrobatic move in which you kick high and hard with one leg, hooking the ball over your head. You end up on the seat of your pants.

You can practice the overhead volley by lying on the ground, tossing the ball in the air, and kicking it away with your instep.

The half-volley is an instep kick that's executed the moment the ball rebounds. It takes a keen sense of timing to be able to make solid contact with the ball. Hit early or late, and the shot will go awry.

A key element is to watch the ball as it drops, and keep your eyes riveted to it as you move to kick.

How you position your body determines the ball's trajectory. Lean into the ball as you kick, and you'll get a low drive. Lean back and you'll put the ball into the air.

The overhead volley—sometimes called a scissors kick—is not for beginners.

Ball should strike the front part of the head just below the hairline.

HEADING

Heading, the ability to shoot or pass the ball with the head, is second only to kicking as an offensive skill. It has defensive value, too.

Any part of the head can be used to strike the ball, but as a player new to the sport, it's best to use the front of the forehead just below the hairline.

Some young players are reluctant to head the ball because they're afraid it will hurt. You can help to overcome this fear with this exercise: hold the ball a few inches above your head, drop it to your forehead, and catch the rebound. Repeat this exercise, gradually increasing the distance.

Then have a partner gently toss the ball toward you, and head it back. Have the partner gradually increase the distance of the tosses. You'll find that your confidence builds quickly.

Two things are vital to be successful. First, you must keep your eyes open. As an object comes close to your face, it's natural to want to shut your eyes. You have to learn to overcome this reflex as far as a soccer ball is concerned. Unless you learn to keep your eyes open, watching the ball as it approaches, you can't expect to make contact properly. The headed ball will seldom be on target as a result.

The second important element is to attack the ball as it comes toward you, rather than letting *it* attack you. When you're heading the ball from a standing position, face the ball squarely as it comes to you.

Practice heading with a teammate.

Sink in the knees; tilt your head back. Just before it touches your forehead, thrust your head at the ball; really lunge for it.

Seldom during a game will you be able to keep your feet on the ground when you're heading the ball. You'll have to leap to get it.

Time your leap so that you are at maximum height a split second before the ball arrives. This is much easier said than done, however. A common failing among young players is to jump too late, and the ball ends up striking them on the arms, shoulders, or chest. Proper timing comes from practice.

Take off from one foot when you leap to get the ball. Keep your head and upper body tilted back. Snap your head forward at the moment of impact. If you're shooting, remember you'll be angling the ball downward, that is, into the goal.

When you jump to get the ball, try to keep your arms behind, tucked to your sides. Otherwise, you may push someone, causing a foul.

PASSING AND SHOOTING

Team play is what makes for soccer success. And passing is the essential ingredient in team play.

You can deliver a pass with either foot, your head, a shoulder, or any other part of your body (except, of course, your hands). Your passes can be high or low, soft or hard, long or short.

Generally, short passes are executed with the inside of the foot, while the full instep is used for longer passes. To pass backwards, hop on one foot, and kick the ball back with the heel of the other foot.

The key to successful passing is knowing where your teammate is positioned and in what direction he is traveling, and then leading him with the ball

Use the heel to pass backwards.

Lead your teammate with the ball when you pass. Make him run for it.

so that he can gather it in without breaking stride.

How fast should a pass travel? It depends on the situation. If the receiver is nearby, you may only have to tap the ball. With a longer pass, drive it.

Keep in mind that the farther a pass travels, the greater the chance it will be intercepted. Short and accurate passes, traveling at the appropriate speed, are what to strive for.

Practice passing off a wall. As you run alongside the wall, kick the ball at such an angle that it rebounds into your path. Continue kicking and running.

Practicing with a partner is probably more beneficial. As you jog together several yards apart, pass the ball back and forth. Gradually increase the distance between the two of you. This type of practice not only improves the speed and power of your passes, but your accuracy as well.

A group of three players can work on several different passing drills, positioning themselves in the form of a triangle. Pass the ball in a clockwise direction, then counterclockwise. Vary your passes, beginning with simple along-the-ground kicks, working up to chips and volleys.

Playing two against one is perhaps the best passing practice of all. This enables you to practice what

Two-on-one drills provide good passing practice.

Low shots are usually toughest for a goalie.

is sometimes called a "wall pass." As players A and B advance toward player C, player B passes to A, then sprints past C to take a return pass. In other words, player B has used A as he might use a wall, "rebounding" a pass off him.

If you become adept at passing, you'll be a good scorer, too. After all, a scoring shot is simply a pass beyond the goalie's reach.

The type of "pass" you execute depends upon the kind of shooting opportunity you're presented. There will be times you won't have a chance to trap and kick the ball; you'll only be able to head it toward the net.

Where the goalie is positioned also influences the type of shots you take. Generally speaking, shots to the right or left of the goalie and below waist level are the most troublesome. The goalie has to bend over or perhaps even dive to make the save, which is more difficult than leaping to catch or tap away a high shot.

Keeping the ball at ground level can cause problems, if it's far enough to the goalie's right or left. Sometimes such shots can only be deflected, giving you, the shooter, or one of your teammates, another chance.

Wherever you shoot, have a target in mind. Based upon what's been said above, the lower corners of the net are usually more difficult for the goalie to cover than the upper corners. So, as a general rule, shoot for the lower corner farthest from the goalie.

THE THROW-IN

The throw-in is the method of getting the ball back in play after it has gone out of bounds, and thus it is very important from a tactical standpoint. Every player should be skilled at throwing in.

You must use both hands and deliver the ball from behind and over your head. Both feet must be in contact with the ground.

Spread your fingers and position your hands in such a way that the thumbs almost meet at the back of the ball. Place one foot a stride ahead of the other. Bend in the knees. Lean back.

To get power and accuracy into the throw, snap your arms and wrists forward, and at the same time shift your body's weight from the rear to the forward foot. Some players prefer to take a two-step run-up as they deliver the ball, rather than throw from a stationary position. It doesn't make too much difference which method you use. What is important is that you get vigorous action with your arms and wrists.

Accuracy is just as important as power. Not only should you target on a particular teammate, but you should put the ball right at the receiver's chest, thighs, or feet. If the receiver is moving, that is, trying to elude a defensive player, be sure to lead him with the ball. Make the play as easy for the receiver as you can.

Sometimes a coach assigns a strong-armed player

Use a grip like this when throwing in.

Take a two-step run-up, if you want; snap your arms and wrists forward as you deliver.

to do the throwing-in. Other times there are tactical considerations. Suppose a team is awarded a throw-in near the goal it is attacking. The coach may assign a fullback to execute the throw-in, so as to have a full complement of forwards and wings available. In the other half of the field, the reverse is true.

RECEIVING AND TRAPPING

No matter how the ball comes to you—high or low, along the ground, or in the air—you must be able to stop it and bring it under control as quickly as possible. Once you have the ball at your feet, you're ready to pass, shoot, or dribble.

Sometimes you'll be able to use the inside of the foot to bring the ball under control. But simply sticking the foot out won't do the trick. The ball will hit your foot and rebound away.

To prevent this, your foot must "give" slightly as the ball arrives. Lift your foot off the ground as the ball approaches. At the moment of impact, move the foot backward slightly, about 2 or 3 inches. This cushions the ball's impact; it stops dead. Then you're ready to make your next move.

You can also use the outside of your foot or the

Trapping with the inside of the foot.

Using the outside of the foot.

For a chest trap, lean into the ball; "give" with it; and let it drop at your feet.

sole to receive passes along the ground. The same principle applies: your foot must "give" as the ball makes contact to prevent it from bouncing away.

If you've played any soccer at all, you know that the ball doesn't come to you along the ground very often. It usually arrives in the air. In such cases, the ball has to be stopped dead and brought under control. This is called trapping.

You can trap the ball with your chest, thighs, or feet. Stay relaxed and keep well-balanced as the ball

When trapping, girls are permitted to cross their arms in front of their chests.

approaches. Prepare to "give" a little at the moment of impact.

Suppose the ball has been lofted in the air and is dropping sharply as it comes toward you. Using your chest is likely to be the best way to trap it. Lean back as the ball nears you. At impact, go back even farther, another 3 or 4 inches to deaden the ball. Then simply allow it to drop at your feet.

When the ball comes on a line toward your chest, lean in the other direction, that is, toward the ball. This enables you to deflect the ball toward your feet.

Girls, when trapping the ball at the chest, are permitted to play the ball off their forearms. Cross your arms and tuck your fists to the right and left of your chin. When the ball comes toward you, meet it with your forearms, relaxing the arms at impact. Drop the ball at your feet.

You can use a thigh to trap, too. A ball that's dropping toward you and arrives about waist high should be trapped on the front of the thigh. Lift your leg with the knee bent. Cushion the ball's impact with the top of the thigh, then let it drop at your feet.

High balls can also be trapped with a foot. Extend your leg outward as the ball nears you. Absorb the ball's impact with the instep or inside surface of the foot, deflecting the ball downward.

Trapping with a foot in this manner is a rather advanced skill. As a beginning player, concentrate on developing the trapping skills mentioned earlier in this section.

Stop the ball with your thigh; then let it drop at your feet. Right: High balls can also be trapped with a foot —in this manner.

DRIBBLING

When you dribble, you advance the ball by tapping it forward with either foot. Dribbling is ball control on the run.

Just as a basketball player learns to dribble using the hand farthest from the player who opposes him, so you should learn to dribble the soccer ball using whichever foot is farthest from the enemy player. When you're seeking to drive by an opponent on your left, dribble with your right foot, and vice versa.

When you dribble, you can use either the inside or the outside of the foot. In either case, use the front part of the foot, that is, the part nearer the toes.

Dribbling wih this part of the foot helps you to keep the ball under control—and ball control is of crucial importance. You should not allow the ball to get more than a foot or two in front of you. Otherwise, you risk losing it to the opposition.

As a beginner, dribble at a walking pace, gradually increasing your speed to a slow jog. Make your strides short and quick. Vary the type of dribble: use only the right foot for a series of touches; then use the left; use only the outside of one foot, then the inside; use the feet alternately.

Set up a line of obstacles—sticks or stones or discarded soda cans—about six feet apart. It's a slalom course. With the ball at your feet, weave your way in and out of the obstacles. Change directions, going

A deft dribbling move

Dribbling through an obstacle course like this is good practice.

to the right of the first obstacle on one pass, and to the left of it on the next.

Dribbling not only involves keeping the ball under control and knowing how to vary your pace and direction; you must also be able to feint when you dribble.

When you feint, you pretend you're going to one side of the player who is opposing you. When the player commits himself to that side, you drive by on the other side.

There are countless ways to initiate a feint. For example, when you dip your left shoulder, you give the impression you are going to attack the opponent on his right side. If he "takes" the fake, you zip by him on his left side.

Speed is vital, of course. You have to be moving fast as you approach the opponent, and be able to explode away the instant that he reacts to your fake.

Another way to deceive an opponent is by stopping suddenly, and placing one foot on top of the ball. The opponent's momentum may be such that he is carried two or three paces beyond you. You then accelerate away or perhaps pass to a teammate.

Try to develop the knack of looking away from the ball for a fraction of a second. This can distract an opponent momentarily, giving you the opportunity to swerve by him.

Another method of feinting involves a fake kick. As you dribble downfield and are confronted by an opponent, act as though you are going to play the ball to your left with your right foot. But instead of

Dribbling around an opponent

making contact, lift your foot over the top of the ball. If the defender reacts, use the outside of the right foot to tap the ball in the other direction, to the right, and explode away.

The boldest method of beating an opponent is to slip the ball right between his legs. If you get such an opportunity, don't kick the ball too hard; simply tap it. This will enable you to pick up the ball on the other side and continue your dribble.

When should you dribble? Whenever it's impossible to pass. As you dribble you'll draw opposing players the way sugar draws flies. A teammate is sure to be left unguarded as a result; then you can pass.

It's also smart to dribble when you're on a breakaway and there's only one opponent between you and the goalie. In such a situation, a good dribble can help you to evade the defensive player to get your shot away.

TACKLING

In soccer, tackling means using your feet to take the ball away from an opponent. You're not allowed to use your hands or arms in any way. Nor, in using your feet, can you make any attempt to trip the opposing player. You must play the ball all the way.

The idea of the tackle, of course, is to allow you to get control of the ball. But a tackle can also cause your opponent to send the ball out of bounds, in which case your team will be awarded possession. Or your tackle attempt may lead to a bad pass. It's not hard to understand why tackling is as important to defensive play as kicking is to the offense.

Timing is all-important in tackling. You must make your move at an instant when your opponent does not have full control of the ball. He may be just receiving a pass and the ball is still in the air, or he may be dribbling and allows the ball to get too far ahead of him. That's when to strike. If you tackle when the opponent is in full control of the ball, he's liable to give a feint and swerve right by you.

The front block tackle is used more frequently than any other. It's a foot-to-foot confrontation. Move in as close as you can, striving to get your weight over the ball. Once you've accomplished this, you can sweep the ball away. You're permitted to use your shoulder when tackling in this way.

You can also tackle from the side. The side block tackle, as it is called, is usually made when you and the player you're challenging are moving in the same direction. Move in as close as you can. When you get your weight over the ball, sweep it away.

There is also the slide tackle. It's like the hook slide in baseball. You make a running slide at the ball, tucking one leg under your body, while reaching out with the other foot. Use your toe or instep to kick the ball away.

The slide tackle requires a good deal of practice. If you miss the ball, you can trip your opponent, in which case a foul will be called against your team. Or the opponent might dart right by you as you slide, leaving you helpless on the ground.

Bear in mind that the sliding tackle was brought into prominence by English players, who—England's weather being what it is—usually compete on soft and spongy turf. Sliding on a hard, sunbaked field can be a painful experience.

No matter what type of tackle you use, always keep your eyes on the ball as you make your move; otherwise, you can be deceived by a feint. While the man with the ball has a certain advantage in knowing the moves he plans to make, in most confrontations it's the tackler who's successful.

Determination counts for a great deal in tackling. If your attempt is halfhearted, you're not likely to end up with the ball. And it is control of the ball that you want.

Tackling from the front

Tackling from the side

A sliding tackle

THE POSITIONS

All soccer positions, except goalkeeper, belong to one of three groups. There are attackers, defenders, and midfielders.

Each of these requires special qualities. You should decide the position for which you are best suited as soon as you can.

Attacking players (designated forwards and wings) are expected to do the scoring. Quickness and speed are the chief qualities you need to play in the forward line. You have to have the ability to flash up and down the field faster than any of the other players.

You also must be exceptional in controlling the ball. You have to be able to pass and shoot accurately. You have to be good at deceiving the opposition and screening the ball when under attack. You have to know how to head the ball with skill and confidence.

Players who specialize in defensive positions (and are known as fullbacks) have to be quick and agile, and have the ability and willingness to play an opponent as well as the ball. If you have a powerful body, are aggressive, and don't mind a bone-jarring collision once in a while, then being a defender might be your best choice.

But brawn alone doesn't make for success as a fullback. You also must be able to anticipate where the ball is going to go and act accordingly. You have to be as determined to keep the ball out of the net as the opposition forwards are at getting it in.

Attacking players—wings and forwards—need good speed.

If you don't feel that you would excel as either an attacker or a defender, then consider becoming one of the midfielders (or halfbacks). Midfielders coordinate a team's offense and defense.

Versatility is what's required to be a midfielder. You sometimes play the role of a defender, so you have to have the desire and the ability to take the

Defensive players have to be able to play an opponent as well as the ball.

ball from an enemy player. But a midfielder is also important to his team's offense, frequently triggering an attack.

As this may suggest, it takes more than the average amount of stamina to be successful as a midfielder. Sometimes you will be required to retreat almost as far as your own goal line, but you also have to be able to sprint deep into opposition territory.

No matter what position you play, your duties and responsibilities can vary from game to game, and even from minute to minute during a game. The overall strategy your team is using, the opposition strategy, the score, where your team happens to be positioned—all of these influence what you should be doing at any given moment.

Never forget that soccer is very much a team game. This means that in addition to developing the skills related to your own position, you should also learn the duties and responsibilities of each of your teammates. This enables you to know where your teammates are positioned—and are going to be positioned—at all times. With this knowledge you're able to move and pass the ball in a way that will do your team the most good.

Team play also refers to attitude. You have to be willing to create opportunities for your teammates by decoying enemy players out of position. This is as important as knowing how to pass and shoot.

To be a midfielder, you need stamina and skill as a playmaker.

Goalie's kick triggers team's attack.

THE GOALKEEPER

Trapping, heading, dribbling, and some of the other skills explained in this book are not important to be goalkeeper. It's a job that's completely different. The "keeper," as he's sometimes called nowadays, has to be skilled in using his hands, in catching the ball or tipping it away.

While the goaltender's chief responsibility is to keep the ball from going in the net, he has other vital roles to play. With his passes and kicks to his teammates, he helps to trigger his team's attack. And on most teams, the goalkeeper is a field general, similar to baseball's catcher, shouting instructions and urging on his teammates.

It takes courage to be a goalkeeper, to be able to stand there and handle balls that are traveling at 60 miles an hour or so. Nor can the goalie allow himself to flinch when an opponent on a breakaway comes careening toward him like a runaway bus.

Being tall is vital. The goalkeeper is usually the tallest player on the squad.

The game is not always thrills and excitement for the goalie. The periods of frenzy are interrupted by long intervals of inactivity, when play shifts to the other end of the field. Nevertheless, the goalie has to keep alert. If he fails to keep his mind on the game, he may suddenly be brought back to reality by the whooshing sound of the ball flying by into the net.

You, as the goalkeeper, should take your stance in the center of the goal, about a yard in front of the goal line. Bend your knees slightly. Move with the ball. When the ball is being played on the right side of the field, for example, ease to your right, positioning yourself on a line between the ball and the center of the goal.

There are times when it's advantageous to leave the goalmouth and dash out toward an attacker. You'll have to do this any time an opponent has broken into the open and is racing toward the goal unchallenged.

By going out after the ball, you force the attacker to shoot from farther away. This reduces the shoot-

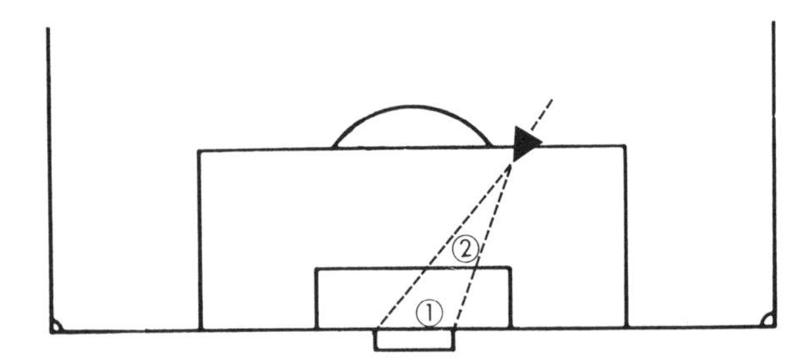

By leaving goalmouth and advancing toward attacking player (position 2), goalkeeper reduces size of target area.

Be sure to get behind the ball.

er's target area (see diagram). But it also gives the opponent an opportunity to swerve by you and take a clear shot. Keep alert.

Whenever possible, you should catch the ball, rather than try to deflect it away with your hands or fists. The first rule in making a catch is to get your body behind the ball. Then if you bobble it, the ball won't be so likely to trickle into the net; your body will block it.

If the ball comes shooting along the ground, get down on one knee in front of it, fielding it the way a baseball outfielder handles a line-drive single. Catch the ball in your hands and arms.

Watch the ball right into your hands. Don't take your eyes off it for an instant. Follow this rule in making catches of every type.

When the ball comes toward you belt high, again get in front of it. As the ball comes into your arms, let your belly absorb the impact. Remember, you don't have to wait for the ball to come to you. You can leave the goalmouth to meet it.

Balls that are high—above your head or higher—are more difficult to deal with. To catch a high ball,

Go up for high kicks . . . down for low ones.

When the ball is too high to catch, deflect it over the crossbar.

you may have to jump for it. As you go up, position your hands so they will be at the back of the ball when you make the catch, not at the ball's sides. Keep one knee raised to ward off opponents who might run into you.

Sometimes a ball will be so high that you won't be able to catch it, but only deflect it. If the ball is almost at crossbar level, leap into the air and deflect it over the bar with your palm and fingers.

You can also use your fists in deflecting the ball. A fist may be the only way to cope with a ball that is booted to your left or right, and too far away to catch. Leap toward the ball; punch it away.

As soon as you've gained possession of the ball, get it back in play as quickly as you can. In throwing the ball, you're allowed four steps before letting it go. (More than four steps results in an indirect free kick for the opposition.) Throw with one hand, keeping the ball low to avoid an interception. And throw hard, as hard as you can.

If you have a teammate who is nearby and not being guarded by anyone, you may want to pass the ball by rolling it. By putting it at his feet, he'll be able to quickly pass the ball or speed away with it.

If you cannot spot an unguarded teammate, you must kick the ball away. The kick resembles a punt in football. Use a three-step approach—right step, left step, punt. Make contact with your instep. Really try to bust the ball. A good kicker will send the ball 40 or 50 yards. Try to target on one of your team-

You can throw the ball to a teammate . . . or punt it away.

mates. If you're successful, it could be the beginning of a scoring thrust.

The penalty kick is the most difficult play of all for a goalie. About all you can do is decide in advance which side of the net the knicker is going to be aiming for. As soon as his foot touches the ball, dive in that direction. If you have guessed right, you have a good chance of making the save. If you guess

Penalty kicks require diving saves.

wrong, don't worry about it. Goalies aren't expected to make saves on penalty shots.

Less of a problem is the corner kick. The kicker usually tries to loft the ball, keeping it about parallel with the goal line. One of his teammates will then try to head the ball into the net.

In defending against a corner kick, take your stance near the goal post farthest from the kicker. Face the kicker. The idea is to dart forward and grab the ball before an opponent can head it.

A final word: as a goalkeeper, always look upon the penalty area as your private preserve, and direct the action that takes place there. When you move out of the goalmouth to make a save, shout out, "Goalie! Goalie!", so as to stop your teammates—the fullbacks, mainly—from playing the ball.

Since you have a better view of the playing area than anyone else, tell the fullbacks which opponents to cover. When you go out to get the ball, instruct a fullback or another player to take over for you in the goal. The ability to direct play in front of the goal is as important to a goalie's success as good hands and quick reflexes.

Perhaps the worst part of playing goalie is the knowledge that you are your team's last line of defense. Make a mistake and it can be fatal. "It's a terrible lonely feeling," Shep Messing, goalkeeper for the New York Cosmos, once said. "It's like being the only survivor on a life raft with sharks cruising on all sides."

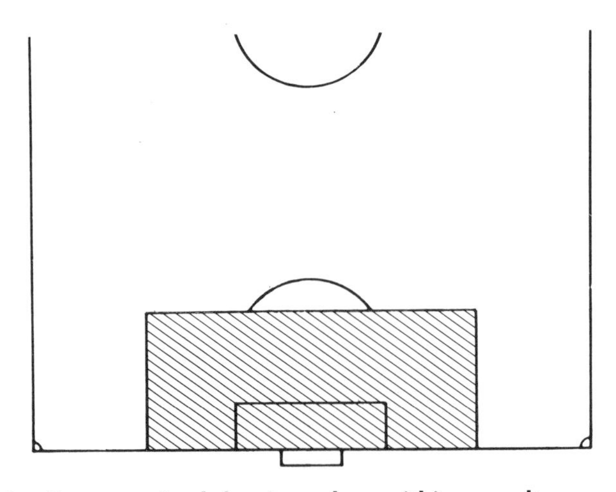

Goalie controls defensive play within penalty area (shaded area).

FORMATIONS

Soccer teams use one of several different tactical formations in order to gain over the opposition.

These formations are defined by numbers. The 4-2-4 and the 4-3-3 are the formations used more frequently today than any others. The first number tells how many players are back on defense, and the second number tells how many players have midfield responsibilities. The third number tells how many players are in the attacking line; they're known as strikers. The goalkeeper is never included, since his duties and positioning never change.

For players learning the game, coaches often rely on the 4-2-4 formation. This means that there are four defensive players (two fullbacks and two halfbacks) stationed across the field in front of the goalie. There are two midfield players (halfbacks) and four strikers (two forwards and two wings).

Since the number of players is equally divided between offense and defense, the 4-2-4 is considered a balanced formation, one that stresses neither offense or defense.

To convert the 4-2-4 to a more defensive formation, it's simply a matter of dropping a forward back, that is, making a linking player out of him. This results in the 4-3-3 formation.

Even greater defensive strength can be obtained

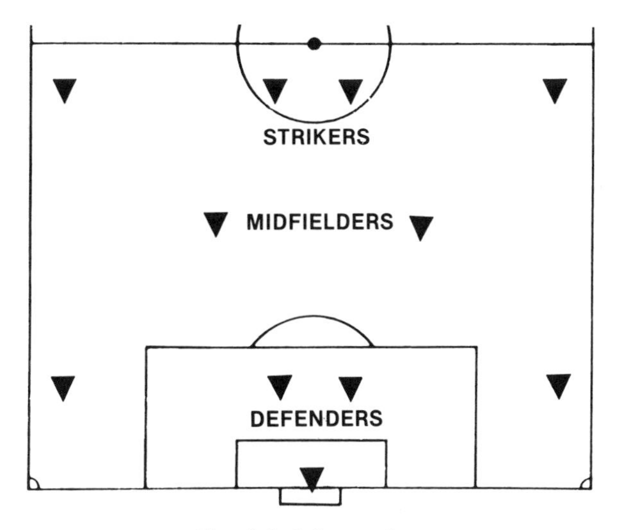

The 4-2-4 formation

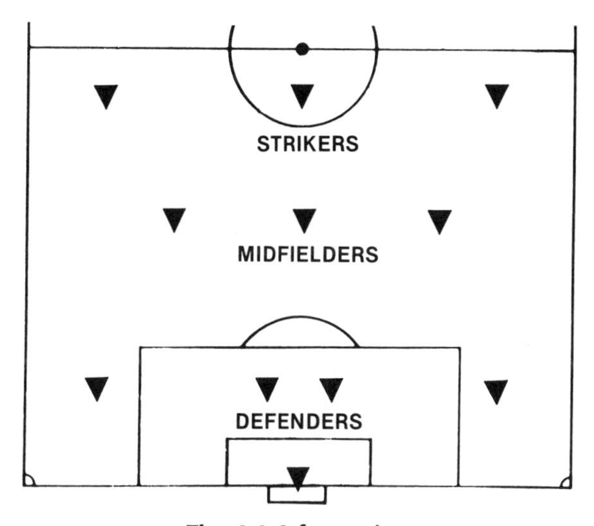

The 4-3-3 formation

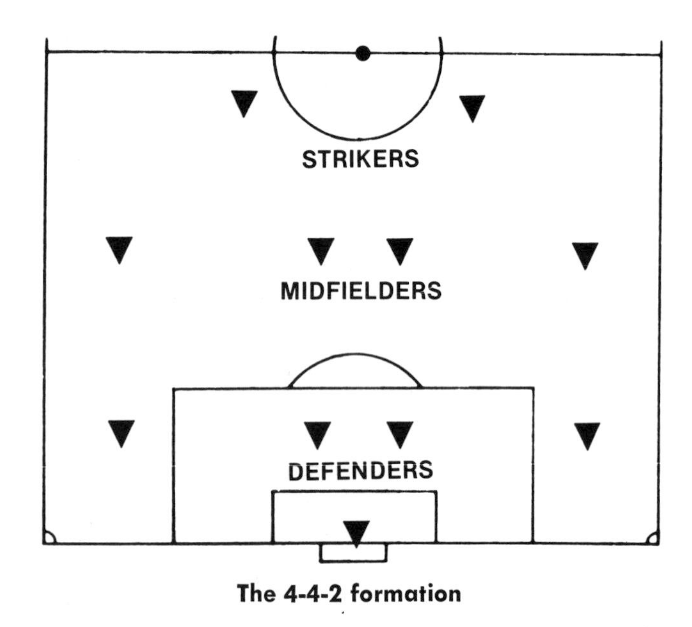

The 4-4-2 formation

by dropping off still another striker. The formation then becomes a 4-4-2. Such an alignment is likely to stifle the enemy attack, but it puts enormous pressure on the two front players.

In the past ten years or so, the game of soccer has changed significantly. Players have to be extremely versatile today. It used to be, for example, that a defensive specialist would be instructed not to cross the midfield line. Not any more. When a team is on the attack today, players can quickly switch responsibilities, with a defensive player moving up to lead a scoring thrust, his defensive duties being taken over by a forward who drops back.

So while the diagrams displayed in this chapter have value as far as strategic planning is concerned, don't expect to look out onto the field and see players aligned in neat rows. Soccer has become too much a game of movement for that.

THE RULES: HOW MUCH DO YOU KNOW?

While the game of soccer itself is easy to understand, sometimes questions arise as to how certain rules should be interpreted. This chapter, which takes the form of a true-false quiz, seeks to answer some of the questions asked most frequently.

Test your knowledge. If you cannot answer more than 10 of the questions correctly, consider yourself no more than a bench warmer. Answer 11 to 14 questions correctly, and you deserve to be a regular. Answering 15 to 18 questions correctly earns you membership on the All-League squad. Get 19 or 20 right and you should think of yourself as an MVP.

The questions begin below. The answers are at the end of the chapter.

1. The ball is deflected off an attacking player and rolls toward the goal, touching the goal line. But before it can cross the line, the goalkeeper boots it away. Has a goal been scored?

2. You're on a breakaway, roaring down on the goal, now only a few yards away. Just as you shoot, an enemy player makes a desperate leap, and manages to get a hand on the ball. But the ball trickles into the goal. What is the ruling here? Have you actually scored?

3. You've been awarded a penalty kick. You get away a powerful boot, but the shot is high, hitting the crossbar and rebounding back toward you. You kick again and the ball goes into the goal. Have you actually scored a goal?

4. Another penalty kick situation. This time you, as the kicker, gently tap the ball forward. It travels only a few feet. Into the penalty area races one of your teammates, and kicks the ball into the goal. Is it a legal goal?

5. The ball is being played close to your goal but outside the penalty area when an opposing player trips one of your teammates. The referee's whistle blasts. Your team is awarded an indirect free kick, and you're assigned to do the kicking. You accidentally boot the ball past your goalkeeper and into the goal. Is it a score for the opposition?

6. You're the goalkeeper. The ball is kicked to your right. You make a diving leap and just manage to catch the ball. But before you can get to your feet, the kicker charges in and kicks the ball out of your hands and into the goal. Is it a legal goal?

7. Your team has been awarded a throw-in. You're positioned near the opposition goal, with only the goalkeeper between you and the goal. The ball is thrown to you. You boot it directly into the goal. "Offside! Offside!" shouts a member of the

opposing team. Are you actually guilty of an offside violation?

8. Again you're the goalkeeper. A penalty kick is at hand. Just before the kick is taken, you move your feet. If the kick is good, will a goal be awarded?

9. Your team has won the toss, and you've been assigned to handle the kickoff. You boot the ball ahead several feet to a teammate, but seeing the ball is not going to reach him, you rush up and kick it a second time. Is this legal?

10. You're sprinting down one side of the field, looking for a pass. Your teammate boots the ball to you. But the ball strikes the referee. Should play be stopped?

11. You're the goalie. Play is at the opposite end of the field when a member of the opposing team gets off a long kick, and it comes rolling toward the penalty area. You go out to meet the ball. When you pick it up, your feet are within the penalty area, but the ball is outside it. Is this a legal play?

12. In the fury of play in front of the goal you're defending, you've slipped to the ground. An enemy player, the ball at his feet, is headed for the goal. As he goes by you, you manage to lash out with one leg, kicking the ball out of his control, but also tripping the man. Is this a legal play?

13. Play is in the front of the goal you're defending when the opposition commits a major foul, giving your team a direct free kick within its penalty area. You're assigned to do the kicking. Eager to get the ball away from your goal, you pass back to your goalie, who picks up the ball and punts it far downfield. Is this a legal play?

14. A shoelace breaks during a game, and you leave the field to get a new one. You re-enter the field just before a throw-in, a play on which your team scores. But the opposition protests that the goal is not good because you failed to report to the referee when coming onto the field. Does the goal count?

15. During play in front of your team's goal, the goalkeeper comes out of the goal in pursuit of the ball, and instructs a fullback to take over for him. One of your teammates takes a shot, but the fullback blocks it with his hands. Is this a legal play?

16. You're dribbling the ball close to the touchline, when an opposing player charges from one side in an attempt to tackle. You veer toward the line, and for a brief period the ball is partly outside the field of play, but also partly on the line. Is this a violation?

17. You're hurrying toward your opponent's goal, the ball at your feet. A teammate breaks into the open and you pass to him. But the ball strikes a dog

that has run out onto the field, and one of the opposition players is able to get possession as a result. Is this a legal play?

18. You have the ball at your feet and you're bearing down on the goalkeeper. An opposition fullback is also between you and the goal when you shoot. The shot goes in. But one of your teammates was closer to the goal than the fullback at the time you shot. Is this an offside violation?

19. Your team has been awarded an indirect kick from a spot about 7 or 8 yards from the opposition goal, and you're assigned to do the kicking. Before play restarts, players from the opposing team line up shoulder to shoulder on their goal line, forming a "wall" to protect the goal. Is this legal?

20. Just as the game is ending, one of your teammates charges into an opposing player within your team's penalty area, giving the opposition a penalty kick. Play is extended to allow time for the kick to be taken. Your team's goalkeeper manages to deflect the kick, but an opposition player boots the ball into the net. Is this a legal goal?

ANSWERS

1. No. For a goal to be scored, "the whole of the ball" must cross the goal line between the goal posts and the crossbar.

2. Yes, it's a goal. If a defending player deliberately deflects the ball with his hands or arms and the ball goes into the goal, a goal is legal. If the ball does not go in, a penalty kick is awarded.

3. No. On a penalty kick, you, as the kicker, are not permitted to kick the ball a second time until it has been touched by another player.

4. Yes. The rules state that in the case of a penalty kick the ball must only be kicked forward and travel "the distance of its circumference"—25 to 28 inches. It is then considered in play. Both of these were fulfilled in the example cited above, and thus one goal counted.

5. No. The referee awards the opposition a corner kick.

6. No. This is considered "dangerous play." The referee should award your team an indirect free kick.

7. No. A player cannot be offside on receiving the ball directly from a throw-in. The goal stands.

8. Yes. The referee makes no ruling until the kick is actually taken. If a goal is scored, he awards it. If the kick is missed, he rules that another kick be taken.

9. No. On kickoffs (or on receiving throw-ins,

corner kicks, or goal kicks), the rules prohibit a player from kicking the ball a second time before it is touched by another player. In the situation described here, an indirect free kick will be awarded the opposition.

10. No. "Play on" is the ruling should the ball rebound off the referee or linesman when they are in the field of play.

11. No. The rulebook says that the goalie is not permitted to use his hands outside the penalty area. In the example here, a direct kick would be awarded the opposition from the point of the infraction.

12. Yes. If you kick the ball first, and the opponent happens to trip over your outstretched leg, the play is absolutely legal. However, if you were to have kicked the opponent first, before clearing the ball, then indeed you would have committed a penalty offense, and a penalty kick would be awarded the opposition.

13. No. On a kick from within the penalty area, the ball must first be kicked outside the area before it can be kicked by another player.

14. Yes, the goal is good. But because you did not report to the referee, the opposition team will be awarded an indirect free kick.

15. No. The fullback, even though he has assumed the goalkeeper's role, has no legal right to touch the ball with his hands. Your team will be awarded a penalty kick.

16. No. To be out of play, the ball must completely cross the boundary line, whether it be a touchline or a goal line. This rule applies whether the ball is on the ground or in the air.

17. No. Whenever the ball strikes what the rules call an "outside agent"—an animal, a spectator, or some other object—the referee will halt play and drop the ball at the point where the incident occurred.

18. No. Since the teammate did not interfere with play nor seek to gain any advantage by his position on the field, there is no offside violation.

19. Yes. When an indirect free kick is awarded a team less than 10 yards from the opponent's goal, opposing players are permitted to stand on the goal line and between the goal posts.

20. No. The extended period of play ended at the moment the goalkeeper deflected the ball.

GLOSSARY

AMERICAN YOUTH SOCCER ORGANIZATION (AYSO)—An independent organization of approximately 9,000 teams and more than 100,000 individual members, ages 7 through 18, that provides competition on a state (about 20 states are represented), regional, and national basis.

BACK—A player with primarily defensive responsibilities. Frequently assigned to cover an opposition wing.

BREAKAWAY—A game situation in which a player in possession of the ball has cleared the last defending player and bears down on the goalkeeper.

CENTER CIRCLE—The circle at the center of the field having a radius of 10 yards with the center spot.

CENTER SPOT—A spot at the very center of the field. The ball is placed on the center spot for kickoffs.

CLEARING KICK—Any kick that sends the ball away from one's goal toward the halfway line.

CORNER AREA—The area within a quarter circle at each corner of the field. Each quarter circle has a radius of 1 yard with its related corner.

CORNER KICK—When a member of the defending team causes the ball to go over its goal line, the ball is put back in play with a corner kick. The ball is placed down within the corner area closest to the area where the ball crossed the goal line, and is kicked by a member of the offensive team. Members of the defensive team must stay at least 10 yards away.

DIRECT FREE KICK—A free kick awarded a team for a serious breach of the rules by the opposition. It can involve handling the ball intentionally, holding, pushing, striking, kicking. tripping, jumping an opponent, charging in "a dangerous or violent manner," or charging from behind. The kick takes place from the point of the infraction. A team can score a goal directly from the kick.

FEDERATION INTERNATIONALE DE FOOTBALL ASSOCIATION (FIFA)—The governing body of soccer throughout the world. Founded in 1904, with headquarters in Zurich, Switzerland, FIFA has a membership of more than 140 different nations.

FORWARD—A member of the attacking line.

FREE KICK—A kick awarded for an infraction of the rules. There are two types: the direct free kick and the indirect free kick.

FULLBACK—See Back.

GOAL—The structure into which the ball must be kicked, headed, or deflected to achieve a 1-point score. The goal is 8 feet high, 8 yards wide, and backed by a net.

GOAL AREA—The rectangular area immediately in front of each goal which measures 6 yards by 20 yards.

GOAL KICK—When a member of the attacking team causes the ball to go over the goal line (but not into the goal), it is put back into play with a goal kick. The ball is placed down in that half of the goal area nearest to where the ball crossed the goal line. A member of the defending team then kicks the ball upfield through the penalty area.

GOAL LINES—The boundary lines at each end of the field.

GOALMOUTH—The area immediately in front of the goal.

HALF-VOLLEY—To kick the ball just as it bounces.

HALFBACK—A player whose primary responsibilities are within the midfield area. Some halfbacks specialize in defense; others excel as playmakers.

HEADING—Passing or shooting the ball with one's head.

INDIRECT FREE KICK—A free kick awarded a team for what is considered a minor offense by the opposition. The offense can involve "dangerous play," arguing with the referee, coaching from the sidelines, or it can be an offside violation. The kick takes place from the point of the infraction. A team cannot score a goal directly from the kick; the ball must first be played by another player.

KICKOFF—The method of putting the ball in play at the start of the game or following the scoring of a goal. The ball is placed on the center spot for an indirect free kick.

LINESMAN—One of two officials who sometimes assists the referee. Linesmen award goal kicks, corner kicks, and throw-ins, and mark where the ball has gone out of bounds.

MAJOR FOUL—A foul penalized by a direct free kick. Major fouls include kicking, tripping, pushing, kneeing, charging violently, charging from behind, and intentionally handling the ball.

MIDFIELDER—A player stationed between the strikers and the defenders; a half-back.

MINOR FOUL—A foul penalized by an indirect free kick. Minor fouls are given for being offside, obstructing, "dangerous play," interfering with the goalie when he has possession of the ball, coaching from the sidelines, and, in the case of the goalkeeper, taking more than four steps with the ball in his possession.

NORTH AMERICAN SOCCER LEAGUE (NASL)—Soccer's principal professional league, with 22 clubs operating in the United States and Canada (as of 1978).

OFFSIDE—A rule stating that when a ball is passed to a player, he must have two opposing players (one is usually the goalkeeper) nearer to the goal than he is. A player cannot be ruled offside if he is within his own half of the field, nor does the offside rule apply if the ball is first touched by a defending player, nor when a player receives the ball directly from a goal kick, a corner kick, or a throw-in.

PENALTY ARC—A segment of a circle that has a radius of 10 yards with the penalty spot as its center.

PENALTY AREA—The rectangular-shaped area at each end of the field which measures 18 yards by 44 yards. The goal area is located within the penalty area.

PENALTY KICK—A direct free kick awarded a team when the opposing team commits a major foul within the penalty area. The ball is placed on the penalty spot. All players on both teams must leave the penalty area, leaving only the goalie to defend.

PENALTY SPOT—A mark 12 yards from each goal and equidistant from the sidelines. The ball is placed on the penalty spot for a penalty kick.

REFEREE—The official who supervises play; he keeps time, awards penalties, and judges when goals have been scored.

SAVE—A blocked shot by the goaltender.

STRIKER—An attacking player; a forward.

TACKLING—Using one's feet to take the ball from an opponent.

THROW-IN—The method of putting the ball back in play after it has gone over a sideline. It is a two-handed, over-the-head throw, with the thrower standing outside the field of play.

TOUCHLINES—The sidelines; the boundary lines at each side of the field.

UNITED STATES SOCCER FEDERATION (USSF)—The governing body of soccer in the United States. Promotes the game with schools, colleges, and associations. Provides standard rules of play and sanctions tournaments.

UNITED STATES YOUTH SOCCER ASSOCIATION (USYA)—A division of the United States Soccer Federation, charged with developing, promoting, and administering the game of soccer among American players 19 years of age and younger.

VOLLEY—To kick the ball before it touches the ground.

WING, WINGER—An outside forward.

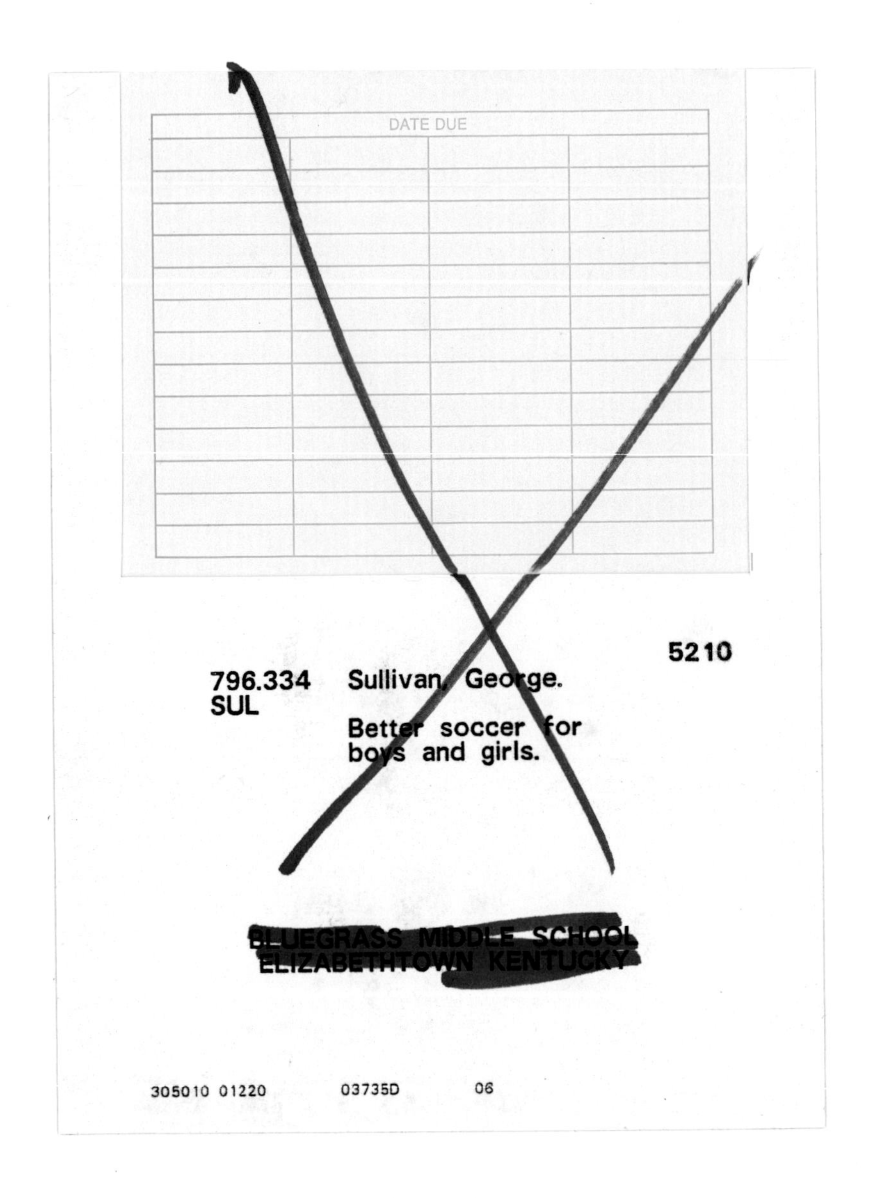